END
OF
THE
LINE

Janice May Udry
pictures by Hope Taylor

Albert Whitman and Co.

Cary was very lucky. She had a grandfather who had all the time in the world to do things and go places just with her. They took long walks and visited the museums and the library, the parks and the zoo.

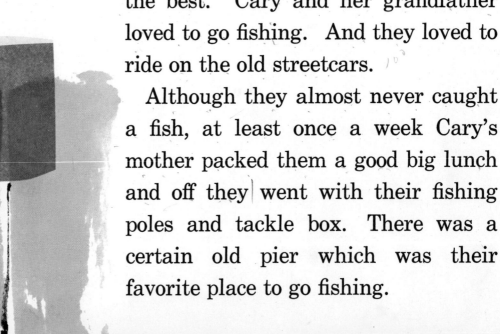

But of all the things they did, there were two things that they liked to do the best. Cary and her grandfather loved to go fishing. And they loved to ride on the old streetcars.

Although they almost never caught a fish, at least once a week Cary's mother packed them a good big lunch and off they went with their fishing poles and tackle box. There was a certain old pier which was their favorite place to go fishing.

On other days they rode all over town on the rusty, dusty creaking old streetcars. Cary's grandfather had once been a streetcar conductor and ever after was allowed to ride free.

All the conductors were their friends. They always greeted each other with a "Hi, Charley!" and "How you been, Tom?" "How-do, Cary. Climb aboard!"

While Cary and her grandfather shared their apples or their bag of lemon drops, the conductors told about the news and any funny happenings along the line.

As a matter of fact, Cary and her grandfather were sometimes the only passengers on the streetcar because, more and more, people preferred the new buses that whizzed past the old streetcars. Why this should be, Cary could never understand. She thought that a streetcar was worth a couple of buses anytime.

One day after they had been fishing all afternoon, Cary and her grandfather walked up from the beach to the corner where they waited for the streetcar.

"Humph," Cary heard Grandfather say, more to himself than to her. "Won't be any natural resources left around here. Nothing but people."

Cary was very curious. "Natural resources?" she asked.

"Oh," said Grandfather, "fish and wild animals and trees—those are natural resources. Take fish. There's no fish living around that pier anymore. And I think I know the reason."

"Why?" asked Cary, sitting beside him on the bench. She was watching the way the sunset was turning the street and the shops pink.

"The ocean bottom there is flat and sandy. Nothing at all left to attract a fish. No shelter of any kind. There needs to be something a fish can make a home in before he'll stay around. About the same as people, I guess. Well, here's Tom. A couple of minutes slow today, Tom!" called Grandfather, waving his tackle box.

He and Cary climbed up onto the big old streetcar.

Tom only nodded to them while he made change for another customer.

"What's the matter?" Grandfather asked him. "You look kind of glum." He offered Tom a lemon drop.

Tom shook his head.

"Haven't you heard the news?" he asked, sighing heavily.

"What news?" asked Cary's grandfather.

"They're going to scrap the streetcars, Henry!"

"Scrap the streetcars?" exclaimed Cary and her grandfather.

"You heard me," said Tom, clanging the old streetcar's bell fiercely. "The city's going to turn 'em into junk. Every last one of them! It's the end of the line for the streetcars."

At home Cary and her grandfather ate dinner in silence.

"What's the matter with you two?" laughed Cary's father. "No fish today?"

"You both look as if you're pondering the world's weightiest problems," said Cary's mother. "Have some more meat loaf, Grandfather."

"No, thank you," said Grandfather. "I'm not very hungry." Then to himself he muttered, "Scrap!"

"What did you say?" asked Cary's mother.

"Scrap!" said Cary. "They're going to scrap the streetcars," she told them, putting down her spoon.

That night Cary had a strange dream. Like most dreams it was mixed up, but mostly it had to do with a family of fish—all dressed up like people and getting on a streetcar!

The next morning Cary laughed when she remembered the dream. She lay in bed for a while thinking about it. Suddenly she jumped out of bed and ran down the hall to Grandfather's door.

"Grandfather!" she shouted. "Are you awake? I've got a wonderful idea!"

She knocked on the door. "It's about the streetcars, Grandfather. Get up. We've got to go down to the mayor's office!"

Grandfather opened his door. "The streetcars, Cary? What's your idea?"

That very morning Cary and Grandfather went down to the mayor's office. But they had to wait and wait a long everlasting wait outside the mayor's office.

They were glad that they had thought to take sandwiches and a Thermos of milk along.

"Mayor Olson will see you now," the secretary finally said.

"What can I do for you?" asked the mayor after they had introduced themselves.

"It's about the streetcars," said Cary.

"Yes, miss?" said the mayor. "They're going to be scrapped, you know."

"Yes, sir, we know," said Cary. "And my grandfather and I don't think that that's the right thing to do at all."

"Is that so?" asked the mayor. "Well, I tell you they've served their usefulness. Nobody ever rides them anymore. We've got fine bus service in our city. The streetcars aren't good for anything but junk now."

"We think they could be useful," said Cary eagerly. "We think the streetcars could increase the natural resources here around Oldport."

"Increase the natural resources?" asked the mayor, puzzled.

"Streetcars?"

"Yes," said Cary.

"What natural resource?" asked the mayor.

"More fish," said Cary.

TO
THE MAYOR'S
OFFICE

Early one morning two weeks later the lighthouse keeper in Oldport Bay stuck his head out the window. Then he rubbed his eyes. "What's going on?" he wondered.

On their favorite pier stood Cary and her grandfather. A crowd had also gathered to watch the U.S. Navy and men from the Fish and Game Department hard at work. They were lowering the streetcars of Oldport into the bay!

"Now that's more fitting," said Grandfather serenely. "There's plenty of usefulness in the old cars yet."

Just then the mayor strolled out to them on the pier.

"That was a mighty fine idea that you and your granddaughter here brought me," he said, watching the work with satisfaction.

"As soon as I found from the Fish and Game Department that making shelter has been found to increase fish population I got busy. They said that streetcars, with all those windows to go in and out of, you know, would be ideal. Even got the Navy to help," he added with pride. "Well, there goes the last one down."

Cary was wondering what the fish would think. She pictured them nosing curiously in and out of the cars that had carried people for so many years. She thought of them drifting in under the exit signs and out again where it said "Enter Front Only."

"They'll be fish hotels," she thought.

"Wait a minute," said Grandfather suddenly. "Did you say that's the last one they're lowering now?"

"I did," said the Mayor.

"Well, it's not!" said Grandfather firmly. "That's five that've gone down to the fish. How about old Number Six?"

The mayor's eyes twinkled. "Get in my car. I've something to show you in City Park."

Cary and Grandfather rode uptown with the mayor.

There they found old Number Six. It had a new coat of paint and was standing near the middle of the park, not far from the library.

"What's the sign over the door there say, Cary?" asked Grandfather.

"Why, it says 'Streetcar Conductors' Clubhouse,' " exclaimed Cary. "And look, Grandfather, they are planting flowers and shrubs all around it."

"Well, Mayor," said Mr. Michael. "This is a fine thing. Wait till I tell Tom and Charley!"

"We're planning a little celebration tonight," said the mayor. "The band will play and the ladies are serving lemonade and cookies. Would you make a little speech, Mr. Michael, in honor of the occasion? Something about the history of the streetcars?"

"Yes, I will be happy to," said Grandfather proudly. "There's no one knows more about them. I'll be glad to speak, Mayor."

That evening under a big moon the city park, gay with party lanterns, was filled with people. Everybody came for the opening of the Retired Streetcar Conductors' Clubhouse.

While Grandfather, in his old uniform, made his streetcar speech, Cary sat on the front row beside her mother and father and all the old streetcar conductors.

And ever after that, the streetcar clubhouse was a cheery place for people to meet and chat a while whenever they were downtown.

Cary and the other children often skated, walked, and bicycled to the old streetcar after school. It was always a good place to get warm around the little stove on cold days, and there was always a good supply of apples and lemon drops.

And in the summer, the Oldport pier became famous for the abundance of fish that lived in the waters of Oldport Bay.